Little Elephant's Trunk

ISBN-13: 978-0-545-11586-5
ISBN-10: 0-545-11586-8

Text and illustrations copyright © 2006 by Hazel Lincoln. All rights reserved.
Published by Scholastic Inc., 557 Broadway, New York, NY 10012,
by arrangement with Albert Whitman & Company.
SCHOLASTIC and associated logos are trademarks and/or registered trademarks of Scholastic Inc.

12 11 10 9 8 7 6 5 4 3 2 1   8 9 10 11 12 13/0

Printed in the U.S.A.   40
First Scholastic printing, September 2008

Little Elephant's Trunk

Written and
illustrated by

Hazel Lincoln

SCHOLASTIC INC.
New York Toronto London Auckland Sydney
Mexico City New Delhi Hong Kong Buenos Aires

All over the land there was great excitement. It was springtime, and springtime meant babies . . . babies everywhere.

The chimpanzee's baby clung tightly to its mother.

The giraffe's baby nuzzled its mother's face.

The tortoise's baby struggled out of its shell.

The hippo's baby took
straight to the water.

The zebra's baby
hid in the long grass.

And the springbok's
baby ran and ran.

The elephants had a new baby, too.
The whole family rumbled with pleasure as they
gazed lovingly upon Little Elephant.

Little Elephant took his first wobbly steps and fell.
Something long and gray was tripping him up.

He struggled to his feet—and it happened again! But now his mother was calling.

The herd was going to the river.

Little Elephant hurried alongside his mother, stumbling as he tried to keep up.

He slipped down the riverbank and fell with a loud splash into the water.

He looked down. A face looked back at him. And something odd dangled from the middle of the face. The strange thing was a trunk!

Then he realized. He was looking at himself—at his own reflection!

What was the strange dangling thing for?

Little Elephant didn't know, but he did know that he was thirsty.

The zebra was drinking the water, but Little Elephant couldn't do that. His trunk got in the way.

He looked at the big elephants. They dipped their trunks into the water, put them into their mouths, and . . . drank.

Little Elephant dipped his trunk into the water, put it into his mouth, and sucked carefully. The cool water was so good!

Now the sun was burning down.
The tortoise was shaded by his shell, but Little Elephant didn't have a shell.

He looked at the big elephants. They were using their trunks to spray water over their backs.
This looked like fun!

Little Elephant trumpeted with delight as he joined the elephant shower. But now the herd was moving to their feeding ground on the far side of the river.

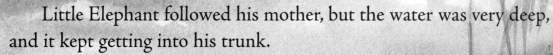

Little Elephant followed his mother, but the water was very deep, and it kept getting into his trunk.

In panic, he scrambled back to the bank.

The chimps swung across the river on vines, but Little Elephant didn't have any hands.

He looked at the big elephants. They all had their trunks sticking up out of the water.

They were breathing by snorkeling!

Little Elephant crashed into the water, thrust his trunk toward the sky, and paddled happily to the other side.

When he came out of the river, he sank into
thick, deep mud. The mud felt good in the hot sun,
and he longed to cover his body with it.

The hippos, with their short legs, wallowed in
the mud. But Little Elephant's legs were too long.

He looked at the big elephants.
They picked up large dollops of mud with
their trunks and threw them over their backs.
Little Elephant tried it. He splattered the
cool mud over himself.
It felt wonderful!

The herd was on the move again, pushing their way through the long grass.

The grass was so high that Little Elephant couldn't see where he was going. He was afraid that he would lose his mother.

The springboks leaped over the grass with their graceful legs as they followed their mothers, but Little Elephant's legs were thick and heavy. They were not made for jumping.

He looked at the big elephants. They walked in a long line with Grandmother in the lead. Using its trunk, each elephant held the tail of the one in front.

Quickly, Little Elephant lifted his trunk and grasped his mother's tail. Now he felt safe.

At last the elephants reached the feeding ground. Little Elephant spotted some juicy-looking leaves, but they were just out of reach.

The giraffes with their long necks nibbled delicately at the leaves, but Little Elephant's neck was very short.

He looked at the big elephants. They curled their trunks around the leaves, tore them off, and put them into their mouths.

After a little practice, he could reach the lowest leaves with ease. Delicious!

The sun had started to dip below the horizon. It had been a long day for Little Elephant. He was very tired.

He snuggled up close to his mother and felt something gently stroking him.

It was her trunk.

He curled his trunk around his mother's. *What a very useful thing a trunk is after all!* thought Little Elephant.